STARSHINE AND SUNGLOW

Betty Levin

Illustrated by Jos. A. Smith

GREENWILLOW BOOKS, New York

98820

Library of Congress Cataloging-in-Publication Data
Levin, Betty.
Starshine and Sunglow / by Betty Levin ;
illustrated by Jos. A. Smith.
       p.   cm.
Summary: Kate, Ben, and Foster attempt to protect their
neighbors' corn from the animals by setting up two scarecrows,
whose changing clothes and positions provide them with
distinct personalities while keeping pests away.
ISBN 0-688-12806-8   [1. Scarecrows—Fiction.
2. Corn—Fiction.   3. Farm life—Fiction.]
I. Smith, Jos. A. (Joseph Anthony) (date), ill.   II. Title.
PZ7.L5759St   1994   [Fic]—dc20
93-26672   CIP   AC

FOR
MAGGIE AND DAN
AND
GREG AND RAFIQUE

BEFORE

Every spring, after the frost is out of the ground, Mr. and Mrs. Flint plant a crop of sweet corn. All their neighbors take an interest. So do the red-winged blackbirds, who like to tweak the first green shoots that poke up through the earth. So do the crows, especially later in the summer when the ears grow plump on the stalks. The crows perch on nearby branches to spot the corn; they call to one another in harsh, eager voices, noting the progress of the coming feast. Some crows probe through the green husks as soon as the kernels form.

But the raccoons bide their time. Only when the kernels are perfectly ripe do they come at night to raid the corn plot. After they have sampled one ear here and one ear there, after they have downed this stalk and that, they leave before daybreak.

In the morning Mr. and Mrs. Flint pick whatever remains of the good ears. Most of the corn is tossed in the pickup and driven across town to be sold at a farm stand. But some corn is always left in a bushel basket in the shade of an apple tree, where the neighbors on Flint Farm Road can stop to get today's corn and to leave money for it in the soup can that hangs from the lowest branch.

Often the children are sent to bring home the corn before the day grows warm. The fresh tender ears are best when kept cool, as everyone on Flint Farm Road can tell you. All the neighbors are experts on sweet corn. How can they go wrong with their daily supply? Who wouldn't take an interest in the bushel basket under the apple tree and in the corn plot where those green-sheathed ears ripen?

1 *The three of them* had finally settled on something to do this afternoon. As usual Kate and Ben charged ahead. As usual Foster lagged behind. They were the only real children on Flint Farm Road. Kate's older brothers and Ben's little sister didn't count, because they couldn't or wouldn't join in any of the children's projects. Today the three were on their way to let Mrs. Flint know about their favorite kinds of corn. There was probably still time before she went off to buy her seeds.

Just before they met up with her at her mailbox, Mr. Torpor came slouching out of the woods way down behind the corn plot. Tall and bent, he moved stiffly as he peered about him. Ben and Kate slowed to give him time to greet Mrs. Flint and go on his way. They had a funny feeling about him. His was the only house on Flint Farm Road that was always dark at night when all the others had lights in their windows.

As Mr. Torpor passed them, he nodded without speaking. He was carrying some kind of pad or book. His field glasses hung from a strap around his neck.

Mrs. Flint looked up from a letter she was reading. When the children told her why they had come, she shook her head.

"No corn this year," she told them. "We're giving up."

"No corn!" exclaimed Ben. "It's our favorite thing."

"Your families can buy other people's corn at the farm stand," Mrs. Flint said. "It just isn't worth it for us anymore. It's a losing battle. We can't fight the critters."

The children understood that the critters were all those creatures that came uninvited to feed on the crops.

"But you grow enough for the critters," Kate said. She was thinking of the words Mrs. Flint always chanted as she dropped the seeds into the soil:

> One for the blackbird,
> One for the crow,
> One for the raccoon,
> And one to grow.

Mrs. Flint nodded. "But every year the critters keep taking more than their share. No matter how hard we fight, we keep losing."

"It sounds like war," said Ben.

"And so it is," Mrs. Flint told him. "First we get the air strikes. Squadrons of red-winged blackbirds. Then come the crows with their sneak attacks. And finally, just when we think we've made it to harvest, the raccoons hit us with their slash-and-burn tactics."

"The raccoons burn?" exclaimed Kate. "How do they do that?"

Mrs. Flint sighed. "That's only in a manner of speaking. What they do," she explained, "is ruin what they don't eat. That's how they've won."

"But they'll lose, too," Ben argued, "because there won't be any corn for them, either. You'll lose because you won't have corn to sell, and we'll lose because Flint Farm corn is the best corn in the world."

"Maybe so," Mrs. Flint replied, "but what's to be done?"

The children gazed across the road at the big, sloping field of ryegrass. Way up in the far corner, where the bare trees bounded the open land, Mr. Flint's tractor chugged and rattled as he began to plow the ryegrass into the earth. That was where corn for the cattle was grown.

"What will you feed the cows?" asked Kate.

"Oh, we'll still grow field corn to put in the silo. Raccoons or not, we can't do without it. But as for the sweet corn . . ." She spread her hands. "We just have to cut our losses."

The children looked over the corn plot with the stubble still showing from last year's stalks. Then they said good-bye to Mrs. Flint and headed home.

2 *"Everyone took* the corn for granted," said Ben.

Kate repeated Mrs. Flint's words: "What's to be done?"

"We have to get all the neighbors behind Mr. and Mrs. Flint to change their minds."

Kate glanced up toward Mr. Torpor's house, the nearest one to Flint Farm. "How do we get the grown-ups on our side? Especially," she added, "him."

Ben frowned. Mr. Torpor liked to paint pictures of cows and of Mr. and Mrs. Flint working on the farm. Ben had never seen Mr. Torpor doing anything else. "Well," Ben answered, "he's home a lot. So we can ask him just to be on hand."

"On hand for what?" Kate demanded.

"For whatever Mrs. Flint needs to keep the critters away. Maybe he can stand guard," Ben added, remembering that this was like a war.

Kate made no comment. She was trying to imagine Mr. Torpor marching back and forth in front of the corn plot.

The children trudged on. When they came abreast of Kate's house, they paused.

"Anyone home?" Ben asked her.

She shook her head.

"We'll go to my house," Ben declared. "My mom knows how to organize things."

They found Mrs. Addario mopping up something awful from around Daisy's high chair.

"No corn this year?" Mrs. Addario exclaimed. She listened to Ben's idea about getting the whole neighborhood to help. Then she lifted Daisy out of the chair. "No harm trying," she said. She carried Daisy through to the hall and called back to them, "But we mustn't leave the Flints in the lurch. It's up to you kids to be sure people understand what's expected of them." She paused at the foot of the stairs. "I hope you're not biting off more than you can chew."

"Chewing makes me think of corn on the cob," Ben said. "I was going to ask for the kind with the big yellow kernels."

Kate said, "I like the mixed-up yellow and white kind." She turned to Foster. "What's your favorite?"

He shrugged. He didn't really know. Then he said, "I like the names best. Butter and Sugar. Peaches and Cream. Sunglow. Miracle. Starshine."

"You can't eat names," Ben told him. "Still, it's good you know so many of them. It'll get people thinking about what the corn tastes like. We'll go to everyone on the road and take a survey and write down what kind of corn they want. Then we'll tell them they won't get it unless they promise to help."

Kate said, "Maybe we should get our own families first. Then we'll be able to tell the others we've already got half the people behind us."

Ben nodded. "So we each go to our parents. And then what? Do we go to the others together, or divide up?"

"I can do Miss Ladd," Kate offered. Miss Ladd lived next door and farther back, almost in the woods. Sometimes Kate helped her weed her rock garden and ran errands for her. Long ago Miss Ladd had been a dancer. Now she was stiff and slow and walked with a cane. Her house smelled of thyme and rosemary and other herbs. A hummingbird fed at her window. Kate and Miss Ladd once sat in velvet, round-backed chairs for more than an hour to watch the tiny bird poised, its wings whirring, until Kate could sit still no longer. "I mean," Kate went on, "I'll ask her to help, but I don't really know what she could do."

"The main thing is to get everyone to say yes," Ben told her. "Later we'll find out what kind of help is help." He rushed on. "I'll talk to Mr. and Mrs. Josephson. I'm not afraid of their dogs."

That left Mr. Torpor. Kate and Ben eyed each other. Then they looked at Foster.

Foster looked straight back at them. He didn't offer to speak to Mr. Torpor. He didn't refuse to, either.

"Maybe we should all three go together," Kate suggested. "I mean, since we don't know him all that well."

"Or send a grown-up," Ben put in.

But first there were the other mothers and fathers to convince. There was no time to waste if there was any hope of getting the corn planted this spring.

3 *Kate's parents* gave her a hard time. They didn't think it mattered much where they got their corn. All the farm stands carried local produce. Anyway, the corn season didn't last very long.

Then Kate's oldest brother spoke up. The Flints' corn was one of the things he would always remember about living so close to a real farm. Kate's mother gave him a fond look. The year after next he would be off to college and maybe gone for good. So she said something to Kate's father about the connection with home. After that they agreed to support the Flints. "Within reason," added Kate's father. "Within reason," echoed her mother.

Next Kate dropped in on Miss Ladd, who was in her small kitchen making tea and toast.

"Is that what you have for supper?" Kate asked.

"It is what I sometimes have for supper," Miss Ladd answered in her careful way.

Kate thought of all the times she delivered fresh corn to Miss Ladd's front door. "But later, in the summer and in the fall, you have corn on the cob, don't you? Fresh from under the apple tree."

Miss Ladd said that nowadays she scraped the kernels off the cob with a knife and then ate them with a fork. Corn was delicious that way.

Kate thought it was a strange way to eat corn, but she knew

better than to say so. Instead she told Miss Ladd that the Flints were giving up the sweet corn unless everyone banded together to help protect the crop from the blackbirds and crows and raccoons.

Miss Ladd nodded and nodded. The toast grew cold in the toaster. The steam that had plumed from her teapot spout thinned and vanished. Then she said, "I'm all for neighbors joining together for the common good, but I don't think I'd be very useful. You know how little I get about."

"You could help right away," Kate blurted, "if you speak to Mr. Torpor for us. We don't know him that well."

Miss Ladd went straight to the telephone and called Mr. Torpor. "Frank," she said, "could you spare a moment? I'm just making tea. Come and have a cup." She sounded polite, but her tone left no room for refusal.

By the time Mr. Torpor appeared at her door, the kettle was bubbling again, and Miss Ladd was handing Kate a plate of thin ginger biscuits to take into the parlor. Miss Ladd followed with three cups and saucers on a tray. Without being asked, Kate returned to the kitchen for the teapot. It gave her something to do while Miss Ladd explained the situation to Mr. Torpor.

He ate three ginger biscuits before responding. Then he said, "At the height of the season I live on corn. But I won't go along with any shooting. I won't help if it means doing in the animals."

"No one is asking you to shoot at them," Miss Ladd declared. "We're asking you to outwit them."

Mr. Torpor looked startled. "Me?"

"You and everyone else. We must be cleverer than they."

Mr. Torpor handed over his cup to be refilled. When he had drained his second cup of tea, he rose to his feet. Standing, he seemed too tall for the parlor's low ceiling. "I suppose you may count on me," he said, "but you must know that I'm limited in my resources."

"Nonsense, Frank," Miss Ladd retorted. "I'm sure you have hidden depths."

Mr. Torpor drew up his shoulders in a kind of shrug that gave him the look of a long-legged bird.

When the door closed behind him, Miss Ladd beamed at Kate. "Your plan is launched," she declared. "And I rather think he hasn't an inkling that it's being run by three kids."

"Would he mind if he knew?" Kate asked. After all, he was bound to find out.

Miss Ladd had no idea. "Poor man," she said, "he never recovered from his hasty marriage. The wife and her four children moved in with him. Six months later they all moved out, never again to be seen on Flint Farm Road. That was a long time ago," Miss Ladd added, "but I expect he's been shy of children ever since."

Kate hoped that she and Foster and Ben didn't remind Mr. Torpor of those long-ago four children. At least he was on their side now. They had Miss Ladd to thank for that.

4 *Ben had to wade* through two dogs and three cats to get inside the Josephson house. Mr. Josephson was polite, but he didn't seem glad to see Ben. "It's Ben Addario," he shouted to his wife. "Looking serious." He turned to Ben. "Raising money for some cause?"

His wife called up from the cellar, "You handle it."

Mr. Josephson heaved a sigh and reached for his checkbook. "So," he asked, "what's the pitch?"

As Ben informed him, Mr. Josephson stepped backward, his hands upraised as if to fend off Ben's plea. "We sail on weekends," he protested. "We cruise most of August. Sorry about the corn crop, but as you can see, we're out of the picture."

Mrs. Josephson emerged from the cellar. She held a pan. "I have to mix up some more food for the puppies," she said. "Can't you deal with Ben?"

"Puppies?" Ben exclaimed.

"I am," Mr. Josephson said. "I just did deal with him. I explained."

Mrs. Josephson asked Ben if he'd like to see the puppies. She sent him a searching look. Now that the puppies were eating real food, she had a problem getting them fed during the day when she and Mr. Josephson were at work. "I don't suppose you'd be interested in looking in after school and feeding them?" she wondered.

"Would I!" Ben told her. "Can Kate and Foster help?"

"We'll see," Mrs. Josephson replied. "Come watch me fix the food. You may as well learn how."

The puppies were in a pen beneath the cellar window. They wiggled and jumped on one another and stepped in their pan of food and then came skidding over to visit Ben. They were black-and-brown curly-coated creatures that looked like toys.

Ben was so enthralled he almost forgot his errand. It was only when Mrs. Josephson started to spell out the exact rules for taking care of these puppies that he found a way back to his task.

"We'll come every day after school if you join our neighborhood plan to save the corn."

Mrs. Josephson looked doubtful. "Corn?"

"Mr. and Mrs. Flint," he explained, "have declared war on the critters that attack their corn. We have to help. It's all or nothing."

Mrs. Josephson frowned. Maybe she didn't believe in war.

"See," Ben added, "we neighbors will be the peacekeeping force." If only another TV news phrase would pop into his head. But nothing else came to him. "Peacekeeping," he repeated, his voice rising.

"We aren't around very much," she said to him. "I don't see how we could be useful."

"We need to get everyone behind the Flints. That's all. Then they'll start the corn. Then they'll tell us what we can do."

"Well, of course we're behind them," Mrs. Josephson replied. "We can certainly offer moral support."

Ben was quick to accept this much. Mrs. Josephson hunted around for an extra key and then warned him not to lose it. The dogs pranced between them, their nails clicking on the wood floor, their hairy muzzles upthrust and eager.

"Which one's the mother?" Ben asked.

Mrs. Josephson pointed. "This one."

But the dogs looked so much alike that Ben lost track of which was which.

Mrs. Josephson said both dogs would be closed away in an upstairs room when he came to feed the puppies. Otherwise they would steal the puppies' food. Even as she spoke, one of the dogs darted down the cellar stairs. Mrs. Josephson charged after it.

Mr. Josephson walked Ben to the front door, saw him out, and shut it firmly behind him.

5 *Foster Baring lay* on his stomach, reading. Downstairs his father and his father's friend Adele talked together in the kitchen.

"How about setting the table?" Dad called up to Foster.

Foster nodded. "In a minute," he said into the book.

"Foster? Did you hear me?"

Foster shut the book and rolled off the bed. "Yes," he said as he made his way down to the kitchen.

Dad handed Adele a glass of wine and started toward the

living room. But Adele didn't follow him. Foster guessed she was going to try to get him talking.

"Anything new at school?" she asked.

Foster pressed the napkins hard to make them lie flat. "Not really."

But Adele wouldn't let it go at that. "After school?"

About to repeat himself, Foster stopped short. He still had to speak to Dad about this corn thing. "Mr. and Mrs. Flint are giving up corn," he said.

"Giving up what?" said Adele.

"No way," his father retorted from the living room. "Raymond Flint's already plowing."

"That's for the cows," Foster explained. "They're giving up the Butter and Sugar and Peaches and Cream kind of corn."

Foster's father returned to the kitchen. He said, "They might as well cancel August and September."

"Is it too much work?" Adele asked.

Foster shook his head. "It's because of the red-winged blackbirds and the crows and especially the raccoons. They're taking more than their share."

"Well, then," said Foster's dad, "I suppose we'll have to think about planting our own."

"Where?" asked Foster.

"I don't know. Somewhere. It doesn't have to be big like the Flints' plot." He and Adele talked about it some more. Then they went outdoors to look for a space that could be dug up and planted. When they came back inside, Foster's dad was saying, "Well, what do you suppose is the smallest size plot that would work?" And by the time they sat down to supper, he had shifted to offering the services of his print and copy shop in case someone else decided to start growing corn.

"We could make signs," Adele suggested. She worked with Dad in his shop.

Foster imagined signs with arrows saying: BLACKBIRDS— THIS WAY. He doubted that anyone on Flint Farm Road was going to try to do what Mr. and Mrs. Flint had done so well for years. If they couldn't beat the critters to the corn, who else could? But all he said to his father and Adele was that everyone was supposed to lend a hand. If Mr. and Mrs. Flint thought the whole neighborhood was behind them, they might try one more time.

Foster's father said it was a bit unrealistic to expect people who worked all day to be able to help. But Adele pointed out that any project that got Foster to open up like this and share with them was worth their support.

So Foster's dad finally agreed. Sort of. "We'll do what we can," is how he put it.

Adele tried to keep Foster talking about the neighborhood plans, but he couldn't think of anything else to tell her. "There's Seneca Chief," he said, searching back to last year's crop for other names. "And Seneca Starshine."

Then he had to explain to her that these were varieties of sweet corn. When she asked him what each of them was like, he was at a loss. He could only go on naming them: "Stardust, Golden Bantam, Honey and Pearl . . ."

6 *Late Saturday afternoon* everyone who lived on Flint Farm Road, except Kate's brothers, turned out to show that they were united against corn-eating critters. Kate's father had to drive Miss Ladd, because it was hard for her to walk even that short distance carrying a jar of her famous corn-and-pepper relish. The rest of the neighbors chatted as they walked together and took turns pushing Daisy in her stroller.

There was never much traffic on Flint Farm Road. Most drivers coming from the highway were taking a shortcut or else they were lost. But some people just liked driving this way because of all the fields and woodland leading to the farm. After that came the houses on the uphill side of the road: first Mr. Torpor's low house on the ridge, then the house that belonged to Kate's family; next, set back toward more woods, Miss Ladd's house painted barn red, and finally the big house where the Josephsons and their dogs lived. Across from them, on the downhill side, were the Addarios and, right after them, almost within shouting distance, Foster's house.

When everyone was gathered on the Flint porch, Miss Ladd presented the corn-and-pepper relish to Mrs. Flint.

"Look, Raymond!" Mrs. Flint exclaimed. "It's your favorite."

Mr. Flint, who was leaning wearily against the porch railing, kept his eyes on his old dog, Bramble. Ben's little sister,

Daisy, clutched a fistful of Bramble's hair and was trying to put it in her mouth.

"Thank you, Miriam," he said to Miss Ladd. "I hope it's not your last."

"It is," she told him. "There won't ever be another jar like it if I have to get my corn at the farm stand now. But," she added, "if it's too much work to keep up the sweet corn, we don't mean to push you."

"Yes, we do," Ben whispered to Kate. "I thought you said Miss Ladd was on our side."

Kate whispered back, "She is. I think."

Mr. Flint shrugged. He stooped down to Daisy. Very gently he pried her fingers open and beckoned to Bramble to move aside. But Bramble just thumped her tail and let the baby crawl over her. "I don't know," he said to everyone. "It only seems like too much work when it comes to the losses. We appreciate you coming over like this. But unless someone has a shotgun and excellent aim and all the time in the world, there's no stopping the ravages."

"But Raymond," Mrs. Flint put in, "a scarecrow usually works for a while. So did that spotlight we set up. It just didn't cover enough ground."

"Birds get used to scarecrows," he said. "Raccoons get used to lights."

"Couldn't we try all sorts of different things?" Ben blurted. "Everyone would help."

"Without a gun?" asked Mr. Flint.

"This is supposed to be a war without any shooting," Kate told him.

Mr. Flint smiled. "Nice idea," he said.

She could tell he didn't think it made any sense.

"Anyway," he went on, turning to his wife, "it's really up to you. I'll go along with whatever you choose to do. Only right now I'm afraid I've got to finish feeding up the cows."

Mrs. Flint stopped him. "You know perfectly well it takes two of us to bring the sweet corn along. So it should take two of us to decide." She held the corn-and-pepper relish up to the late sunlight.

Half turned, Mr. Flint paused and eyed the jar. "That your vote?" he asked her.

Mrs. Flint nodded.

"So," he replied. "Corn it is."

Everyone on the porch said, "Ah." But they could hear him muttering about the pesky critters as he stumped off to the barn.

"We're with you, Raymond," Mr. Addario called after him. "With you all the way."

Mrs. Flint said, "He's grateful, really. It just gets harder to keep things going here. We're cutting back the herd again. We want to take things easier."

"You should cut back," Mrs. Josephson agreed. "We thought you would when you switched from dairy cows to beef." She turned to the others on the porch. "I don't think any of you were here when the Flints were milking morning and night."

Mr. Torpor untangled his long legs and straightened up.

"I don't mean you, Frank. I mean the younger neighbors."

"Well," said Mrs. Flint, "we appreciate our neighbors, old and new." Bending down to Daisy and Bramble, she plucked the baby off the dog. "And this newest," she went on, "may have her first taste of sweet corn come August. If we're lucky," she added. "If the weather holds and if we really do beat the critters to the crop."

7 *The rest of the* weekend was a washout. Dense clouds spread gloom and then rain. It soaked the land and brought all soil preparation to a halt.

On Monday the children went straight from the school bus to the Josephson house to feed the puppies. Kate wanted to stay and play with them, but Ben insisted that they check up on the corn plot.

"You can't hurry the weather," Mrs. Flint told them when they showed up. "It'll take a few days for the ground to dry out."

"We only came to see if you needed help yet," Kate said. She sent Ben a look that meant he'd better act as though that was what he had in mind.

"That's right," he chimed in. "That's what we came for."

"Well, then, let me see." Mrs. Flint thought a moment.

"We'll set up a scarecrow as soon as we sow the seeds. Maybe if it had a change of clothes from time to time it would keep the birds edgy. So you might collect some raggedy things for the scarecrow."

The children went to Ben's house and were making a good start collecting things when Mrs. Addario stopped them.

Ben clutched a sweatshirt. "It's full of holes," he argued. "You told me not to wear it anymore."

"It can be patched," Mrs. Addario explained. She made two stacks of clothes out of their collection. One was of good outgrown things to be saved or passed on to younger kids. The other was of clothes to go to a shelter for homeless people. There wasn't one item of clothing left for the scarecrow.

As soon as Mrs. Addario carried off the things to keep, Ben whispered, "Let's try Foster's house. I bet no one cares what we take from there."

"And don't try Foster's house," Mrs. Addario called down to them. "What applies here applies all over. It's a matter of principle not to waste usable clothes."

"So what can we do?" Ben shouted back. "Mrs. Flint asked us for stuff and we're trying to help."

"Why don't you get donations from all the neighbors?" his mother responded. She was back downstairs for the load for the shelter. "Ask for things on their last legs or clothes that can be left outdoors for a while. They'd be on loan, to be returned."

Ben groaned. "No one's home to ask."

"Your mom is," Kate said.

"Yes," Mrs. Addario agreed. "I'll make the first donation." She marched right back upstairs and was gone for a while. When she returned, she was carrying the bottoms of curtains that had been shortened, spreads that had been ripped beyond repair, threadbare sheets, and sleeves that had been cut off a shirt.

The children spent the rest of the afternoon inventing outfits for the scarecrow. Foster came alive when they asked him to draw stick models wearing the scraps and bits to see what they'd look like. At first he just recorded Ben's and Kate's arrangements. But pretty soon he was inventing his own effects with material he just dreamed up.

That evening the three of them made the rounds of all the households. They were so organized by then that they even remembered to ask for safety pins to hold the clothes together.

"No needles and thread?" asked Miss Ladd.

"If it needs sewing and is worth mending," Kate explained, "we're not allowed to use it for the scarecrow."

Miss Ladd handed over a few colorful strips of cloth left from her quilting.

The last stop was Mr. Torpor, who said he didn't have anything he didn't need. After all the stuff they had collected from the other houses, that was hard for the children to believe.

Kate peered past his door into his front room. It was perfectly empty. Ben stared, too. "Thanks anyway," he managed to say.

"There's nothing to thank me for," Mr. Torpor replied

dryly. "I'll try to think of something for next time you come by. I'll have to look around."

But what could he find in that spotless room? Kate wondered. Was his kitchen like that, too? In her house there were pots and jars and message pads and magazines and lots of magnetic gadgets holding lists and recipes and cartoons on the refrigerator door. She couldn't picture Mr. Torpor's kitchen like that, not after seeing his bare front room. No wonder the windows facing the road were always dark. There was nothing inside to light up. Nothing at all.

8 *Finally the day came* for planting the corn. On the big field across the road, the seed was drilled into the ground by machine. But in the plot for people corn, the seed was sown by hand, and not all at once.

The plot was mapped out in blocks for each variety of sweet corn. Mrs. Flint showed the children how to set the seeds, four at a time. "One for the blackbird," she recited.

"That's actually a red-winged blackbird, isn't it?" said Ben.

"One for the crow," she continued with a nod. "One for the raccoon," she declared as she counted out the third kernel, "and one to grow."

Ben had the first turn. He got silly over the chant and began to mix up the words and fool around. Mrs. Flint made him leave the sack of seeds and stand outside the harrowed plot. She pointed to the spot where he had flattened the furrow and messed up the row.

"Do I have to say all that stuff?" he demanded. "Can't I just plant?"

"Of course you can," Mrs. Flint told him. "Just count out four seeds at a time."

So Ben straightened out the row he had kicked. Then he finished sowing the seeds.

When it was Foster's turn, he reached into the sack of Silver Queen corn seeds and gazed at the white, dry kernels lying in his palm. As he went about his planting, he kept his voice so low the others could hardly hear his words. They sounded like the rustle of leaves brushed by a hand, light as the milky corn silk that by and by would sprout from each silver ear.

Downhill from the plot and around behind the house young cattle crowded at the gate. They could tell that Mr. Flint had left the big field to haul silage down to them.

By the time Foster had finished sowing his block of Silver Queen, there was such a racket from the tractor and the cows that when it was Kate's turn, she had to shout the words at the top of her lungs. She wanted all the red-winged blackbirds to hear, and the raucous crows, and the raccoons holed up in their hollow trees. They had to get the message that they could take their share of corn and no more. NO MORE.

9 *Every school day,* after the children took care of the Josephsons' puppies, they hurried to the corn plot, only to find it brown.

Ben stared at the great expanse of earth with nothing showing but many small stones and a few clumps of dead corn stalks that had escaped the plow. "Maybe something ate the seeds," he said.

Kate glanced across the road to the field. It looked the same, only bigger—a huge, brown nothing. She shook her head.

Ben heaved a sigh. "Growing stuff is boring," he declared.

They went back to play with the Josephsons' puppies.

A few days later two flappy scarecrows faced each other across the corn plot. One wore a hat. The other had a mop head with strings for hair. Each was dressed in tattered barn clothes.

It was hard to believe that any hungry red-winged blackbird would take these scarecrows seriously. The birds were bound to catch on fast that the scarecrows were just dummies.

The children went back to sort through their collection of clothes and rags. They would be ready when they were needed.

After that nothing happened. There was no sign of corn and no sign of blackbirds, although Mrs. Flint had said they arrived north well ahead of spring.

Mrs. Flint told the children not to check every day, or it would take longer. But it was hard to stay away.

Mr. and Mrs. Josephson put the puppies out in a pen behind their house. When the children went to feed them there, the puppies nearly burst through the gate. They were so much bigger now that they wanted to chase one another. They wanted to chew on socks and shoelaces and the children's hair. They took more time than ever.

One day it rained. Ben decided the puppies should be taken inside to their pen in the cellar. It was hard to catch each drenched and squirming puppy without losing any through the gate. But Kate found a way to bring them running to her; she called, "Pup, pup, pup," just the way she did when she brought their food.

When Mr. and Mrs. Josephson came home, they called Ben to thank him. Ben told Kate and Foster, "I hope they remember how we helped when the time comes to ask them for help."

"I thought we did it for the puppies," said Kate.

"Of course we did," Ben agreed. "And for the Josephsons."

Foster opened his mouth and then shut it again without speaking.

The next day, after the puppies were fed, the three children trooped over to the Flint Farm for another look. At first glance everything seemed the same. But when they cast their eyes over the big field, they were startled by a strange kind of light that seemed to brush the slope with a green tinge. They couldn't actually see anything growing, but the green light cast its bloom over the entire field.

They drew close to the corn plot. Ben dropped to his knees and peered at the soil. "Look!" he cried. The other two bent over. They saw a tiny wormlike bud inside a crack in the earth.

They sat back on their heels. They looked about and found that while they had concentrated their attention on this one plot of ground seeded with corn, changes had gone on all around them. The apple tree had begun to bloom, most of the blossoms still tight and red, but a few outer petals already spread like pink seashells. Roadside weeds had sprung up. And at the edge of the woods, new leaves were closing the gaps between the branches. Soon the trees would become a kind of wall dividing the wild from the farmed.

At that moment nothing stirred. The stillness felt as vast as the empty sky. The trees held no birds at all, at least none that could be seen.

At either end of the corn plot the scarecrows stood at attention. Even now, as the farm seemed to draw its breath, they looked ready for action.

"It's like a battlefield," Ben pronounced.

Foster spoke up. "Looks like a peacefield to me."

Anyway, thought Kate, something wasn't just about to happen. It had been happening all along, something unseen that they had helped to start.

10 *The weekend came* and went. So did the puppies. The children watched some of them being carried off in the arms of strangers. One girl around Kate's age let her puppy slip from her grasp. The puppy dashed off, the girl shrieking and chasing after it. Kate, standing in the driveway, called, "Pup, pup, pup," just the way she did at feeding time every day. The puppy scampered over to her.

"It's mine," said the girl. "We just bought it."

Kate handed over the puppy without a word.

The girl's mother spoke from the car. "Thank you for showing us how to call him."

Kate nodded. Never again, she thought. Taking care of someone else's puppies was fine until it ended. Then it was just plain awful.

Ben said, "Come on. We'll go look at the corn plot."

But Kate didn't want to. "We were just there," she replied glumly as she turned back toward her own house.

Her parents were working in their little garden. Lettuce and radishes were up. Tulips made splashes of red and purple along the flower border.

"Want to help?" her father asked.

She shook her head. Up in her room she flopped on her bed with one of the stuffed animals she used to sleep with. Today it brought no comfort.

Later on her mother looked in and asked if she wanted to invite a friend over.

"I want a puppy," Kate answered.

"You know we can't. No one's home all day."

Neither were the Josephsons, and they had two dogs. But Kate only said, "What's the point of being stuck way out here if we can't even have a dog?"

"There's the farm," her mother said. "You always like going over there. Maybe there's a brand-new calf to see."

Kate didn't want a calf. She wanted a shaggy black-and-brown puppy. But she took off anyway, just in case something was going on at the Flints' barn. On her way she gazed at the big field that sloped up on her left. That was how she came to be the first person to see the red-winged blackbirds descend in black clouds to feed on the new green shoots.

She raced to the farmhouse and pounded up to the door. Mr. and Mrs. Flint were both home. Mr. Flint thanked her for telling him that the blackbirds had arrived.

"What are you going to do?" she demanded breathlessly.

"I'm going to finish my dinner."

"Don't you want to chase them away?"

He shook his head. "They'd just be back."

"Why don't you have scarecrows out there for them?"

"Too big an area," he replied. "It would take an army of scarecrows. And setting them in would do as much harm as the blackbirds."

Mrs. Flint said, "Since we can't beat them, we try to think of them as thinning the rows for us."

"Will they move to the corn plot?"

"Some might. You can wave them away if they do. Wave all you like, only don't step on any of the plants."

Kate raced back along the road to sound the alarm. Ben was stuck watching Daisy for a few minutes. Foster, who was about to be taken shopping, was rescued by Kate. He charged into his house and came running to Ben's with a weapon. It was a butterfly net on a long pole.

"You going to catch red-winged blackbirds in that net?" Ben asked him.

Foster said he was only going to wave it to scare them off.

"I'll get something, too," Ben said. He charged upstairs and came down again holding a flag with a snake on it and some words. "This ought to scare them," he boasted.

Kate read the words: DON'T TREAD ON ME. Maybe the blackbirds would consider it a warning from the corn.

As soon as Mrs. Addario drove up to the house, the three children dashed out to the road. Kate peeled off at her house to look for something she could wave with, too. Her eye fell on the garden rake lying on a stack of empty seed packets. She took the packets with the boldest pictures and speared them onto the rake. Then she joined the boys.

Armed and determined, the three marched to the corn plot. There they waited and waited. A few blackbirds looked as though they might land, but they veered off to the big field instead.

"We're keeping them away," Ben shouted. "We're winning!"

They stayed there waving their butterfly net and flag and rake until Mrs. Flint called from her porch. Mr. Addario wanted Ben to come home. Foster was supposed to go with him. "And you'd better go, too," Mrs. Flint told Kate. "You shouldn't be out here all alone."

"We'll be back tomorrow," Ben promised.

Mrs. Flint said they had done a grand job but that they mustn't let the red-winged blackbirds run their lives.

Kate stopped at home long enough to ask if she could go to Ben's house. Her father started to say that he would miss her, noticed the rake with the seed packets, and finished by laying claim to her weapon and sending her along with the boys.

Mrs. Addario was out. But Mr. Addario produced pizza and let them make their own toppings.

The awful day ended not too badly.

11 *Over the next few days* the ranks of red-winged blackbirds thinned for a while, until a new squadron flew in from the south.

"They think the corn is greener on this side of the road," remarked Mrs. Flint. "I wish they'd think it was greener on the other side of the county."

Kate searched for something to take the place of her parents' rake and seed packets. She came up with the idea of using Daisy's crib gym, which had colored rings and bars dangling from it.

"You may borrow it," Mrs. Addario finally agreed, "if you take it in before any rain."

"But Daisy doesn't use it anymore," Ben argued. "I thought you said she's outgrown it."

"There might be another baby some day," Mrs. Addario informed him.

Later Ben said that his mom only said threatening things like that to keep him in line. "She wouldn't actually have another baby," he insisted. "She hated not being able to bend over. And Dad had to pull her up out of the easy chair." But as they walked along the road, he couldn't keep from casting an anxious glance back at his house.

Kate couldn't figure out how to use the crib gym like a

butterfly net or a flag. She ended up draping it from the arm of a scarecrow.

On Sunday the children found at least two dozen blackbirds in the plot, helping themselves to shoots of sweet corn. They also found Mr. Torpor seated on a log with a pad in his lap and pencils and paints at his feet.

Waving the snake flag, Ben ran, roaring, at the birds.

"What are you doing?" cried Mr. Torpor as the birds took to the air.

"They're eating our corn!" Ben shouted. "We promised to help keep them away. You promised, too."

Mr. Torpor kept on painting for a bit. After he set aside his brush, he said, "It was so peaceful here."

"There's lots more blackbirds in the big field," said Kate. "Can't you paint them there?"

Mr. Torpor shook his head. "I need to see every detail. Here I can be close without sitting in the mud." He showed them his sketch pad with penciled drawings of bird heads and wings and feet and beaks, of feathers and beady eyes. Then he held up the picture he had been painting.

Foster let out a long sigh. He gazed at the pair of birds, one with scarlet wing patches edged in bright yellow. "How?" he asked, crouching in front of Mr. Torpor. "How do you do that?"

Mr. Torpor regarded him with surprise. "I'm not sure I'm able to tell you. I just do."

"Foster draws, too," Kate confided. "He does space stuff, mostly."

Mr. Torpor rose creakily and gathered up his things. "I don't suppose the birds will come back now," he said, staring hard at Ben. Then he walked away.

"Weird," Ben commented in an undertone. He turned to Foster. "Why didn't you ask him why his front room's empty, while you were at it?"

"Ask him yourself," Kate retorted, when Foster wouldn't answer. "Unless you're scared to," she added.

"I'm not," Ben said. "I'll find out. When he's in a better mood."

They lazed around for a while until Mr. Flint came by and announced that two calves had been born during the night. The children surged toward the barnyard, where the mother cows stood as far apart as they could and stared warningly. The calves tottered toward each other. But the one that was still wet kept returning to stand under its mother's chin. The dry one came fairly close, and then skittered away when the newer calf's mother thrust her head at it. The other cow gave a low moan, calling her baby to safety.

"This is what Mr. Torpor should paint pictures of," Kate declared. She turned to the boys, but only Ben was by her side. "Where did Foster go?" she asked. Ben had no idea.

The two of them turned back to the corn plot, where the brown earth with its fine, green-fringed rows was once again dotted with red-winged blackbirds. The invaders looked as though some hand had scattered them there like a fistful of stones.

Ben and Kate broke into a run. When they caught sight of

Foster stretched full-length on his stomach at the edge of the plot, they faltered.

"Foster?" Ben called out.

Foster's head turned sideways. "Don't," he commanded in a voice that scarcely rose above a whisper.

Ben was taken aback. He wasn't used to Foster telling him what to do. Then, recalling why they were there, Ben said, "Those birds are eating our corn plants. We have to chase them away."

"Wait!" Foster whispered. A few birds fluttered nervously and hopped out of range.

Ben toed a stick but moved no closer. "He can't be trying to catch one," he said to Kate. "He doesn't even have his butterfly net."

Ben and Kate waited a little longer. Then Ben announced that they were coming. He led the attack with a rush.

The birds rose in noisy flight. For an instant they were all helter-skelter, black bodies and wings darting and shooting up and sideways. Flashes of scarlet blinked as the low sun caught their brightness like bits of reflecting glass. Then they collected themselves and soared overhead, becoming at last a small black cloud, the red lights snuffed by distance.

Foster sat with his knees drawn up, his head tilted back.

"What were you doing?" Ben wanted to know.

Foster stood up. "Looking," he said.

"Well, we're not supposed to. We're here to chase them."

"They'll come anyhow," Foster told him. "We can't always be here, and we're not human scarecrows."

Ben and Kate had to agree with him. Then they decided it was time to find some scary new clothes for the real scarecrows.

On the way to Ben's house, Foster kept lagging and glancing back. It was almost as if he had forgotten what they were supposed to be doing, as if his mind were somewhere else.

12

The scarecrows began to take on traits of their own. First the tattered old clothes were returned to the barn. Then the scarecrow with the mop head appeared in a skirt made from part of a bedspread. Kate used a lot of safety pins to gather in the waist and leave the skirt full below. Ben found a grain bag to cover the bunchiness in the middle. That helped, although the bag itself tended to spoil the effect.

Two days later the children found that someone had re-placed the grain bag with a real blouse stuffed with newspaper to fill it out. The blouse had big splashy tropical leaves printed on it. No one was surprised that the birds kept their distance.

But Ben minded someone else taking over the scarecrows. "It was our idea," he said. "They should ask us first."

Kate reminded him that everyone was supposed to help. Ben didn't care. Secretly he wished that he had set himself up as commander at the start. That was the best way to wage war against the invaders.

By the end of the week a few of the blackbirds were back, plucking at the tender shoots of corn. Since they seemed to avoid the mop scarecrow standing nearest the house, the children went to work on the one facing her at the far end of the plot.

First they gave him a proper head made from an outdoor broom, with worn, stubby bristles for hair. Mrs. Flint let them have hay-baling twine to tie the broom onto the original scarecrow body. Now he had two legs, as well as a head of sorts, with its funny haircut. Foster painted a face on the bound bristles just above the joint with the broomstick.

Soon the scarecrow with the bristle-cut sported baggy sweatpants and a bright orange towel around his neck. It bothered Ben that he hadn't thought of the towel himself, but he had to admit it looked great. And no red-winged blackbirds visited the corn plot.

There were still plenty of them across the road in the big field. The children caught sight of Mr. Torpor trying to stalk the birds as he sketched them. He didn't get very close.

One afternoon after school, Foster went off on his own. Later Kate saw him with Mr. Torpor way up on the far side of the field near the line of trees. She showed Ben, who said, "I thought Mr. Torpor didn't like kids."

"Maybe he only doesn't like kids that talk," Kate responded.

They checked the young corn plants. There was nothing to chase away. There weren't even very many red-winged blackbirds left in the big field.

But the next time the children looked, they found a crow sitting on the bristles of the broom figure. It was time for another change.

Kate figured the crow thought the broom bristles were like field stubble. She wanted a big hat to cover them.

First the children went to Mrs. Flint. But all she had was a big old straw hat that looked too much like the bristles. Next they tried Miss Ladd, who sent them into another room where there was a carton full of clothes to give away. But there was no hat.

"Maybe Mr. Torpor could spare one," Miss Ladd suggested.

"He doesn't have anything," Ben replied.

"There are things in the back of his house," said Foster.

"Great!" Ben exclaimed. "Did he tell you why the front room is empty?"

Foster shook his head.

"Did you ask him?" Ben demanded.

Foster shook his head again.

"Well, come on, then," Ben told him. He practically dragged Foster after him. "We can ask him about the room when we ask him about a hat."

Kate stayed behind to put things back in the carton. Miss Ladd helped her with the folding. After a few quiet minutes, Miss Ladd said, "I don't think Frank Torpor will talk about his front room."

Kate had a spooky feeling. "Did something bad happen there?"

"Not exactly," Miss Ladd told her. "Yes, I suppose it was bad. Just before he was married, Frank cleaned out that room and another one so that his wife could fill them with her own things. He had to sell his family belongings to make the space.

Then, when she and the children moved out, the front room and the one bedroom were left without a stick of furniture."

Kate asked, "Couldn't he get back his old stuff?"

Miss Ladd shook her head. "As I recall, he didn't have the heart to do much of anything. After all these years, he's never really changed, except that back then he repaired bicycles for a living. Now that he's retired, he lives on his pension and on something he gets for being wounded when he was a soldier, long ago."

Mr. Torpor a soldier! Kate tried to picture him in uniform. She tried to imagine him quick and straight.

Miss Ladd flipped the lid of the carton closed. Seeing the look on Kate's face, she added, "It was his choice. He told me then that he intended to keep the front room stripped as a reminder and a warning never to let anyone else into his life."

Kate was in no hurry to find the boys. She needed a little time alone to get used to Mr. Torpor not being spooky anymore.

13 The next day after school the children trooped down to the corn plot to see what Mr. Torpor had provided for a hat. He had promised Ben and Foster that he would come up with something, even though he refused to stop painting just then.

"You should see all the stuff he has," Ben told Kate. "His house is loaded with paper and cardboard and pots of paint."

"Maybe it's because he has no upstairs for storing things," Kate said.

"Maybe." Ben's voice dropped. "I even got a peek at his room. It's so full of junk I don't know how he gets into bed."

They had their first glimpse of the new hat from the back of the broom scarecrow. They broke into a run so that they could see it from the front and found that it was an old-fashioned helmet with mosquito netting draped around it. Not only that, but the broom scarecrow was wearing a safari jacket with lots of pockets that flapped. A bright red bandanna stuck out of one of them.

From a branch of the apple tree a pair of crows railed at the helmeted figure. This new getup was working, because crows had begun to land in the big field, and yet not one of them came to the corn plot.

Only a scattering of red-winged blackbirds remained in the field corn, where the crows stepped boldly between the rows as they probed for worms and bugs in the freshly turned soil. Squirrels chasing each other around the plants screeched at the new invaders. One squirrel even took up the defense of the apple tree beside the corn plot. Rearing up on its haunches, it chittered wildly at the unwelcome crows.

All the sounds were harsher and louder now. Every creature appeared to be striving to keep something away from every other creature. "Mine! Mine!" they seemed to shriek.

The mop-headed scarecrow stared across the rows of new

plants at the guy in the helmet and safari jacket. Kate thought she looked sort of wimpy now that the broom scarecrow was so well dressed. But before the children could agree on what the mop should wear next, it began to rain.

The following day the rain continued. Everything was sodden. Birds of all kinds dropped down to feast among the corn, but they didn't disturb the plants. The children stayed indoors.

When the rain stopped, Flint Farm was transformed. The big apple tree looked slightly moth-eaten, its gorgeous pink mantle in tatters. Petals lined the stone wall and coated the grass. The corn was visibly taller. And a large red-and-white striped umbrella was opened out over the mop scarecrow.

The children tried to figure out whose umbrella it was, but couldn't guess. "It doesn't mean that we can't do what we want," Kate said to Ben, who was scowling at the thought of grown-up interference. "We need all the help we can get."

They splashed through puddles on their way to Ben's house, where Mrs. Addario brought out an old raincoat that had split down the middle of the back.

"The rain's stopped," Ben informed her.

"We need something bright," Kate put in. "To startle the crows."

Foster eyed the raincoat. "Can I put things on it?" he asked.

Mrs. Addario said she supposed so. She didn't know what Foster had in mind.

After he took the raincoat away with him, Kate and Ben picked over scraps of material. One long checkered strip was raveled at each end. Ben thought they should wrap it around the mop scarecrow's neck for a scarf. Kate didn't think that a scarf would go with the blouse printed with tropical leaves. People didn't wear winter and summer clothes at the same time.

"I bet the crows don't care," said Ben.

"Why don't we just turn it into a belt for her?" Kate said.

They took it to the corn plot to try it on. Foster showed up with the split raincoat, which he had covered with painted stars and planets. The Milky Way stretched from shoulder to hem. Saturn and its rings looked like a target. Foster pointed to Orion the Hunter and the Dog Star. Crows would be leery of hunters and dogs.

The children draped the raincoat over the broom figure's arm. They closed the umbrella and leaned it up against the mop figure. But she needed an arm that would bend. To make one, they rolled up a grain bag and tied it where the joints should be. Once they attached it to the mop scarecrow, they were able to fix her checkered belt so that she looked as though she were waving its fringe at the guy in the safari jacket carrying the painted raincoat.

The children admired their work from every side and corner of the plot. They were so caught up in the effect they had created that they all but forgot about the crows. The broom and mop were poised for action. No one could guess what was likely to happen next.

14 *The children* visited the corn plot almost every day. They had a kind of creepy feeling that something else was going on before their eyes. But it wasn't until they found the broom scarecrow's head uncovered again that they noticed he was no longer at the edge of the plot. He was standing between the third and fourth rows. And he was doffing his helmet at the mop scarecrow, who was also just inside the planted corn.

"It's like a story," Kate declared. "They're trying to get together."

Ben shook his head. "If it's a story," he complained, "we're the ones who are supposed to be making it up."

Foster just stared. Who are these scarecrows? he asked himself. They needed names.

Over in the big cornfield woodchucks surfaced beside their burrows. Whenever Bramble saw them, she barked wildly. The woodchucks scurried back down their holes. Some of them moved on to dogless gardens away from Flint Farm Road. They couldn't tell that Bramble's hunting days were long gone.

Crows came and went, too. The corn had a lot more growing to do before it would seriously interest them.

Meanwhile the scarecrows seemed to have a life of their own. Their wardrobes reflected a new awareness of each other. Kate made a many-colored paper chain to hang around the mop scarecrow's neck. Ben made ears out of old socks his mother had given up trying to mend. He fastened them onto the bristle-headed broom. One ear was pink and one red.

"He caught a fever," Ben explained.

Kate thought the broom was blushing. "Some people's ears get red when they're embarrassed," she remarked.

"That would make both ears red. He caught a fever in the tropics," Ben maintained.

Foster made an earring out of the top of a frozen juice can and hung it from the pink, healthy ear.

Mrs. Flint called from her porch. She wanted them to be careful not to step on the corn while they worked on the scarecrows.

"We know," Ben answered. "Who moved them?"

"Not me," was all Mrs. Flint would tell him.

Some days later they made the rounds of all the houses on Flint Farm Road to ask for new donations. Everyone was aware of what was going on in the corn plot except Mr. and Mrs. Josephson. But they let the children search around in the basement where they kept things that used to belong to their children.

Kate couldn't keep her eyes off the empty puppy pen. But Ben found badminton rackets with a lot of the strings missing and an old stretched-out net.

Back at the farm the children found a broken metal fence post they could shove into the soft earth about midway between the scarecrows, which were now even deeper inside the corn plot. Ben tied one end of the net to the post and the other to a forked branch that they jammed in across from the post. But none of them could figure out how to get the scarecrows to look as though they were swinging their rackets.

"You know what's missing?" said Foster's father when he and Adele stopped by on Saturday morning. "A bird."

Ben, who was struggling to keep one racket propped in the broom scarecrow's hand, said, "We don't want birds. The whole point is to keep birds out of the corn."

"Not that kind of bird," Adele explained. "The bird you hit with the rackets. It's called a shuttlecock."

She and Foster's father went to the barn to look for something. They came back with a few chicken feathers. Now where could they find a Ping-Pong ball?

Kate thought there might be some at her house. Pretty soon her parents and Foster's father and Adele were all sitting on the grass with glue and tape and string, making an oversized badminton shuttlecock. Kate's father supplied a dowel to attach to a scarecrow's hand. The shuttlecock hung from it, far enough from the scarecrow to look as if it were flying toward the racket. The grown-ups insisted that the scarecrows give up the umbrella and raincoat while they were playing badminton. Ben supposed the grown-ups were right, but he didn't like them calling all the shots.

Less than a week later the net had to come down. It got in the way of cultivating, Mrs. Flint told the children. Besides, she said, anyone could see that the scarecrows were coming too close together to play anymore.

That was true. They had moved at least two more times. At this rate they would soon be touching.

15 *The scarecrows* went through more changes of clothes. They began to look like characters out of a very old movie. The broom scarecrow was dressed in plaid slacks and a red blazer with gold buttons. The mop scarecrow sported a one-piece playsuit that prompted Mrs. Flint to remark, "Another time warp. Where did that relic come from? It's practically prewar."

Thinking that she referred to their war against the critters, the children just looked at each other. Wasn't everything prewar?

"It sure didn't come from my house," Ben declared. "We don't do real clothes."

"I've never seen anything like that in mine," Kate put in. She glanced at Foster, who didn't speak. "It doesn't look like Mr. Baring, either," she said.

Mrs. Flint pointed out that whoever was providing the clothes only left them outside for a few days at a time, so no harm could come to them. "And meanwhile," she went on, "nothing's bothered the crop. It's coming along just fine."

The children figured that it wouldn't be like Mr. and Mrs. Josephson to dress the scarecrows. That left only two other households, Miss Ladd's and Mr. Torpor's.

Mrs. Flint shook her head. "Not Frank Torpor's style," she said. "And I can't see Miriam Ladd getting all around these plants with her cane. It takes too much fiddling to rig those scarecrows."

After Mrs. Flint had gone off to help Mr. Flint with chores, Ben declared that the three of them were losing control of the situation. "It's a war, right? Well, who thought it up? We did. We should be the ones in command."

Kate and Foster nodded. They didn't know what to say to him.

Later Kate mentioned to Miss Ladd that Ben seemed sort of jealous of the mystery dresser.

Miss Ladd, who was snipping flowers, laid them in a basket. She said, "It's too bad he can't see what fun someone else must be having."

"Ben thinks it ought to be our fun."

Miss Ladd straightened, her hand at her back. "Sometimes," she remarked, "it's hard for a person to share. What about Foster? Is he jealous, too?"

Kate shrugged. "He never says much."

Miss Ladd asked Kate to water the herbs while she trimmed leaves from the stems of the cut flowers and set them upright in a pail of water. There were pink and white larkspur and dark, velvety red sweet william. There were also a few white peonies with just a touch of red on their petals.

Kate aimed the nozzle at plant after plant to wash away the dusty film that covered the leaves and stems. She soaked the soil all around them.

Miss Ladd came to see and nodded approvingly. "Everything was so thirsty," she said. "I'm sure the Flints are anxious for rain."

Kate shut off the water. She gazed into the pale sky. "Maybe it will come tonight," she said.

"I hope not," Miss Ladd returned. Then she added, "I suppose that's a selfish wish. I only mean I hope the rain will hold off until, say, the day after tomorrow."

"Why?" Kate asked.

"Because," Miss Ladd told her, "tonight is Midsummer Eve. That makes tomorrow Midsummer Day."

Kate's heart sank. How could summer be half over when she still had one more week of school? "I thought summer was just starting," she said.

Miss Ladd nodded. "For you, it is. But for the earth, for all of us on this side of the world, it is the longest day of the year, the time of most light."

Kate could tell from the way she spoke that this meant a great deal to Miss Ladd. But Kate didn't have the slightest idea why.

16

No rain fell that night, and Midsummer morning dawned fair.

Yet everything was changed. The scarecrows, decked out in wedding clothes, now stood side by side facing the road. The broom figure's top hat had slid down over his pink and red ears, but his snappy black bow tie was visible beneath it. The mop scarecrow was swathed in white. Her bridal veil fluttered whenever a car sped by. And in the crook of her

grain-bag arm there nestled a bunch of flowers that Kate instantly recognized.

She tore down the road and off behind her house to bang on Miss Ladd's door.

"You did it!" Kate shouted as Miss Ladd stepped back to let her inside. "How did you?"

"Good morning, Kate," said Miss Ladd. "How did I what?"

"The scarecrows!" Kate blurted. "They're getting married."

Miss Ladd beamed. "A fitting way to celebrate Midsummer. Is there a wedding party?"

"But you know!" Kate insisted. Then she faltered. "Don't you?"

"I can't see the corn plot from here," Miss Ladd reminded her. "I would like to, but I'm a bit shaky in this heat. Maybe when it cools off."

For a moment Kate was at a loss. Then she recalled the wedding bouquet. "What happened to the flowers you picked yesterday?" she demanded.

"Let me think," Miss Ladd replied. "I believe I took all the peonies inside for the table. Didn't I leave the rest out in the pail? I hoped someone might be able to use them."

"Someone did," Kate told her. "The bride is carrying them."

"How do they look?" Miss Ladd eagerly asked. "I hope they don't wilt in this awful heat wave."

"They look fine," Kate said dimly. "I mean," she added, "they're beautiful. It's only . . . only that I don't know who made the wedding happen."

"Never mind," said Miss Ladd. "At least the day is marked with celebration."

And from the number of cars that squealed to a halt as they drove along Flint Farm Road, plenty of drivers and passengers helped to mark the celebration in front of the corn plot, even if most of them didn't have a clue about its being Midsummer Day.

17 *The wedding* lasted one full week. There was no question about its effect on crows and ground critters. The contrasting black and white of the clothes and that fluttering veil kept all would-be invaders at a distance.

Every evening, clouds gathered and thunder rumbled. Now and then a wind swept down from the sloping field and stirred the young corn leaves. They scraped and rattled against each other, making dry insect sounds. Still, not one drop fell. Each morning the sky was cloudless and bleached nearly white.

When the storm finally broke, it caught nearly everyone by surprise, especially the wedding couple. Where was the red-and-white striped umbrella when they needed it? Where was the great split raincoat covered with stars and planets, with Orion the Mighty Hunter and Sirius the Dog Star? Kate thought Ben had put them away and Ben thought Kate had.

Foster said, "Mr. Torpor let me put them in his house."

"In all that junk?" Ben exclaimed.

"It was the closest place," Foster said. "And he didn't mind."

But by then it was too late to protect the wedding couple from the rain. Even after it stopped and the air dried out, their clothes looked so bedraggled and dismal that the children had to think about how to replace them.

"They'd be on their honeymoon," said Kate as she dismantled the wedding gown. "They'd go to the beach."

"Maybe Foster could bring back the helmet and jacket. I bet they're at Mr. Torpor's house, too."

"No," Kate said firmly. "They're going to Bermuda. They need beach clothes."

But when the children fitted out the scarecrows in matching yellow shorts, they looked more than ever like a broom and a mop with extra sticks for limbs. Ben draped a flowery tablecloth around the upper parts of them, but that still left the stick legs showing.

Kate stopped in on Miss Ladd, who suggested that the wedding couple might go on a cruise. There would be dancing every night. Miss Ladd had a closetful of long skirts for Kate to choose from.

"And I might be able to dig up a white dinner jacket from somewhere," Miss Ladd told her. "Though it would probably take a little while."

"I can come back anytime," Kate assured her. "School's done."

Miss Ladd nodded. "That's good news. But I'm just as slow as I was yesterday. Meanwhile, see what you can do with this evening shawl. It goes with the pleated skirt."

So Kate carried Miss Ladd's things to the corn plot to upgrade the mop scarecrow from yellow shorts to formal dancing clothes. The effect was stunning but lopsided, because the broom was still wearing his shorts. Tomorrow she would attend to him, too.

18 *First thing* the next morning Kate started off to see whether Miss Ladd had found a white dinner jacket. But it was Saturday, and Kate's mother was home. She said it was much too early to go visiting. She said Miss Ladd was frail and needed her rest.

So Kate wandered off to the corn plot. There she discovered that a new prop had been added—a suitcase. Now the scarecrows really did look like a honeymoon couple. Kate was still admiring them when Ben showed up.

"Whose suitcase?" he asked her.

"It was just here," she told him.

"Did you look inside?"

She shook her head. "Do you think we should?"

But Ben was already dragging the suitcase forward, laying it on its side, and snapping up the latches. He raised the lid. Inside the suitcase were a white jacket and a maroon bow tie and funny-looking pants that got wide at the bottom.

"They must be special pants for dancing," Kate mused. She was thinking that Miss Ladd couldn't be as slow and frail as she appeared if she had brought the suitcase all the way to the corn plot.

"They're bell-bottoms," said Foster, who had just arrived.

"How do you know?" Ben demanded.

Foster shrugged. "I guess I heard it somewhere." He wasn't thinking about the bell-bottoms, though. He was thinking that the broom and mop had just about everything they needed except names.

When both scarecrows were dressed in all their finery, Kate decided that they needed some glittery jewelry. No one could think which household was the most likely to have any, so the children tried the Josephsons first. But they were away. Even the dogs were gone.

Foster's father was still sleeping, and Ben's mother was no help this time. All she did was warn them to protect all those nice things from the weather.

Miss Ladd just shook her head. She doubted that anyone on Flint Farm Road wore what was known as costume jewelry. "But you ought to be able to make some really flashy things that would scare off the crows."

By this time the crows were far from the children's thoughts. But here was a chance to complete the scarecrows' wardrobe and improve their scariness at the same time. The children spent hours stringing buttons for necklaces and adding old bicycle reflectors, measuring spoons, and spare insulators from the Flints' electric fence.

Once again the Sunday traffic squealed as people gaped from the road.

Kate wondered whether the mop figure was maybe a bit overdressed with all those things dangling from her neck and wrists. She also wondered if anyone would mind if she borrowed a bike reflector to wear around her own neck. Foster said she didn't have to take the scarecrow's; he knew where he could get her some more.

Ben was ready to take a break from the scarecrows. His mother had signed him up for swimming lessons at the pond on the other side of town. He already knew how to swim, but having lessons meant his mother would be sure to get him there. Kate and Foster could come, too, if their parents paid for them. But it looked as though only Kate would join him.

Foster said he had other things to do. He visited the corn plot on his own and brought along one of his father's writing pads and a pencil. Sometimes Mr. Torpor turned up and the two of them sketched side by side. But even when he was by himself, Foster didn't feel alone. All around him living things tracked across the sun-baked earth and rested in the shade of the corn. He saw moles and grubs and dragonflies; he saw crows and chipmunks and earthworms and caterpillars. And he also saw the elegant scarecrows.

They had names now, although no one but Foster knew what they were. The mop one was Starshine. The broom was Sunglow. Whenever he came their way, Starshine and Sunglow seemed to stride out of the corn, arm in arm, to greet him. And each time he settled down to draw the tiny visitors to the plot, he became a part of their busy, hot, green world.

Once he followed the progress of an ant struggling to move

a partly eaten leaf. He was so intent that he forgot to draw. Only after more ants streamed down to help, only after he had watched them carry off their huge prize, only then did he pick up his pad and pencil. After a while he felt the scarecrows' shadows across his back and shoulders. He held up his picture to give Starshine and Sunglow a look at what they missed by standing so tall and partying all the time.

19 *The honeymoon couple* thrived. Before the next rainstorm, someone whisked away the suitcase and set up a big black umbrella that covered both scarecrows. When the sky cleared, the umbrella was removed and the couple, now in plain, everyday clothes, was found standing back among the corn plants. That meant, Miss Ladd told Kate, that the honeymoon was over. It was time for the mop and broom to settle down and look after their farm.

When Kate reported this to Ben, he shook his head. "If they're not all dressed up, how will they scare the crows?"

"Maybe they can put on something that isn't fancy but will work," Kate suggested. She caught sight of Mrs. Flint picking beans. Mrs. Flint was glad to have company and even gladder to have help. She showed Kate how to take each bean without breaking the tender stem. After a while Kate got around to asking her about when she and Mr. Flint came home from their honeymoon.

Mrs. Flint straightened. "We never did have a honeymoon," she finally said. "Raymond's brother was supposed to take over for us, but he broke his arm. So we just stayed home."

"What did you wear at home?" Kate asked.

"Overalls, I guess. We were look-alikes and work-alikes. We milked and fed stock and mucked out."

"Do you still have the overalls?" Kate wanted to know.

That made Mrs. Flint laugh and laugh. "Wore them out, and many more."

"Did you ever get your honeymoon?"

Mrs. Flint went back to picking the long, slender beans. "By the time we had someone who could take over the chores, I was expecting our first child. I didn't feel like going anywhere." She looked at Kate. "I guess you could say we've been here forever. You want the scarecrows to look like Raymond and me way back? Is that what you're getting at?"

"Sort of," said Kate, who wasn't exactly sure.

As soon as Mrs. Flint's basket was brimful of beans, she found four boots with cracked uppers and two old pairs of overalls. One had been cut up to patch other things, but that didn't matter to the broom and mop. Mrs. Flint thought they'd better be moved out of the plot again to protect the growing corn from all the comings and goings. That meant the children had to postpone the change of clothes until Mr. Flint had time to reset the scarecrows.

Well before the next rain, they were standing again at the edge of the plot. The children gave them a pitchfork and hoe.

They looked ready for anything.

When the rain did come, it lasted two long days and then petered out on the third. It gave the corn a big boost, even though many of the lower leaves were spattered with mud. Some plants were as tall as the scarecrows. They were muddy, too. It was a good thing they had been wearing overalls and boots.

After the rain the crows grew bold. They didn't attack the corn, but they dropped down to feed on waterlogged bugs and poked here and there among the arching leaves.

Foster had to go away with his father and Adele. Before he left, he told the other two who the scarecrows were. Then, while Ben and Kate pondered what Starshine and Sunglow should wear next, someone else got to them first. Starshine was back in shorts again, with a striped T-shirt on top. Sunglow wore khaki pants and a blue work shirt. The red bandanna was tied around his head.

"There isn't anything left for us to do," Ben grumbled. He kicked a stone, which bounced off one of the rubber boots.

"We could get them sun hats," Kate said. "Let's look in your house first."

Mrs. Addario gave them lemonade. "Are you sure it's still summer for the scarecrows?" she asked.

The two children stared at her over the rims of their glasses. Didn't she realize that it had to be summer until all the corn was ripe?

Mrs. Addario poured some lemonade for herself. "It just seems," she explained, "that time is different for the scarecrows. It speeds up sometimes, like when they were going out together. It slowed down when they got married."

The children had to agree that most weddings probably didn't last seven days.

Mrs. Addario set down her glass. She rummaged around until she found a straw flowerpot holder. The children tied a ribbon around it. When they stuck it upside down over Starshine's mop head, it would make a fine sunbonnet.

"What can we use for the other hat?" Ben asked.

His mother suggested that they make one out of newspaper. But that was a pirate kind of hat. It was wrong for Sunglow.

Meanwhile Kate mulled over the way time shifted. What did Mrs. Flint mean by forever? Was her life the same every day for years and years and years? Well, not altogether. Not once her kids were born.

Kate tried to remember what Mrs. Addario looked like before Daisy was born. She had special clothes to cover the lump that was Daisy. "Could we borrow some of your pregnant things?" Kate blurted. "We'd be careful. We'll return them."

Mrs. Addario began to smile. "Maternity clothes?"

Kate nodded. Ben started to object. Then he decided it wouldn't hurt to get those things away from his mother.

The two children raced off with Mrs. Addario's lavender print jumper and wads of newspaper to stick inside for a bulge. The sunbonnet topped off the pretty effect. Then they picked a few tiger lilies that grew along the roadside. Ben tied them on Sunglow's arm so that he looked as though he were giving them to Starshine. Kate hung a pail from his other hand.

64

Ben eyed Sunglow. "Is he milking or holding flowers?" he asked.

"First he picked the flowers," Kate answered. "While the cows were coming in. Then he milked. Now he's bringing the flowers and a pail of milk to Starshine."

Ben nodded. His mother drank a lot of milk before and after she had Daisy. Sometimes his father brought her flowers, too.

Kate was thinking what a surprise was in store for Foster when he came home. He had given Ben and her the scarecrows' names. Now she and Ben had something to give him as well.

20

Time not only moved on for Starshine and Sunglow, but for the corn, too. As it grew taller, it filled out. While Starshine's bulge got bulgier, so did the baby ears on the stalks.

When Mrs. Flint heard Ben declare that the battle was nearly won, she had to set him straight. Even though most of the crows had been foiled up to now, the hardest struggle lay ahead. Wait, she warned him, until the crows and raccoons got a whiff of the sweet young kernels.

By the time Foster got home, Starshine was back to her original thinness, and an old baby carriage stood on three wheels in front of her and Sunglow.

Now when some of the cars stopped to take in the scene, people got out with gifts for the scarecrow baby. Mrs. Flint set up a drying rack beside the carriage to display the bibs and plastic toys that had been left.

"Even the outsiders are getting in on our act," Ben remarked.

Mrs. Flint reminded him that everyone was needed. She showed him the corn silk streaming from the early-bearing corn. A sweet fragrance wafted from the sun-struck tassels at the tops of the corn plants. The raccoons were sure to smell it, too. Any night now they might attack.

The children went from house to house to get everybody to meet on the Flints' porch to work out a plan.

Foster's father said he and Adele were too worn out from their vacation. The children stood before them in stubborn silence until the grown-ups said, "Oh, all right. What time?"

The Addarios said they would be there with bells on.

"Bells!" exclaimed Kate. "Bells might be just the thing to scare raccoons."

The Josephsons' dogs barked a lot, but no one came to their door. So the children went on to Kate's house. Only Kate's brothers were home.

"It's Sunday," said the oldest one. "Besides, I never go to meetings."

"Too busy," said the next oldest, who was lying on his back listening to country music turned up all the way to where it made the lamp shades shudder.

Kate knew that awhile back they had both worked in the

Flints' hay fields. She also knew that they had nothing much to do now until the next haying started. "How about lending us that CD?" she asked. "It ought to make the raccoons shake, too."

"No way," said both boys together.

Miss Ladd wondered whether one of Kate's parents could give her a lift to the Flints. Kate explained that she wasn't sure when her parents would be home.

"Never mind," said Miss Ladd. "I'll get there on my own. Maybe I'll stop in on Frank for a sit-down."

"There's not much to sit on there," warned Ben.

Miss Ladd nodded. "It might give Frank a little food for thought. He might have to produce a chair."

At Mr. Torpor's house Kate and Ben retreated behind the hedge.

"So you're home!" Mr. Torpor exclaimed as he opened the door to Foster. "You were gone a long time."

"I know," Foster answered. "There's a meeting this afternoon on the Flints' porch."

Mr. Torpor shook his head. "I'm in the middle of a picture."

Foster just stood there, so Ben stepped forward to say, "It's an emergency. Mrs. Flint said so."

"She did?" Mr. Torpor sounded surprised.

Kate had a feeling those weren't Mrs. Flint's exact words, but she backed Ben up as best she could. "The hardest battle is ahead of us," she reported to him. "The scarecrows can't help."

"Ah," said Mr. Torpor. "That's too bad. I suppose," he

added mournfully, "that means they are finished."

Ben said, "We're supposed to think about raccoons now, not scarecrows."

Even though the meeting wasn't until much later, Kate and Ben decided to get on over to the Flints'. It was clear that Foster wanted to stay with Mr. Torpor, so they left him at the door.

Mr. Torpor invited Foster inside. There were paintings on great sheets of paper strewn all over the kitchen and the crowded back rooms. Foster was used to Mr. Torpor's fine sketches, some of them touched with watercolors, but these pictures were bold and bright.

Foster itched to try his hand at this kind of painting. But where could he spread another sheet of paper? The only floor space left was in the front room.

When he asked if he could work in there, Mr. Torpor nodded absently. Pretty soon Foster was down on his knees trying to paint a scene of the corn plot viewed from the ground.

Later Mr. Torpor stood over Foster and his picture. "How can the turtle stand on the plantain without crushing its leaves?" he asked.

"The turtle's behind the plant," Foster said, "not on top."

His joints creaking, Mr. Torpor crouched down beside Foster. "You can show that this way," he said, using quick, firm strokes of the brush.

Foster sucked in his breath. "Cool," he said. "I didn't know how."

"Actually, you did. You've been getting it with your small drawings." Mr. Torpor flipped the page over. "Try again."

Foster spent the next couple of hours painting in Mr. Torpor's front room. Before he left he took a moment to look at the picture Mr. Torpor was working on. He recognized the green-and-purple corn husks. "Platinum Lady," he said.

"Is that what it is?" Mr. Torpor sounded pleased. "Do you know other names, too?"

Foster nodded. "I can tell you all of them. But I can't find a corn name for the scarecrows' baby."

"Must it have one?"

Foster explained about Starshine and Sunglow.

"Then I'll find you a corny name for the baby," Mr. Torpor promised. "I'll think of it soon."

Late that afternoon the neighbors straggled over to Flint Farm. No one showed much eagerness for waging war against raccoons. Then Mr. Flint told them that already some raccoons were testing the unripe ears on his field corn across the road. He hoped he would be able to scare them off with lights and noise before much damage was done. At least it was possible to protect the sweet corn here if everybody helped the way they had said they would.

Mr. and Mrs. Addario agreed to collect heavy-duty extension cords from everyone and to make sure the connections were safely taped together. Kate said her family would supply a sound system. Foster's father said he would be in charge of lights.

Miss Ladd and Mr. Torpor came too late for this part of the

meeting, but Miss Ladd said they would both do whatever they could. Mr. Torpor seemed surprised that she spoke for him.

Mrs. Flint urged everyone to be ready. If things were in place when the raccoons invaded, the noise and lights might stop them before they took over the plot.

"Are you sure that noise and lights will work?" Ben asked. If only he could think of some backup plan. That would show everyone who was really in charge.

21 *Nearly one week* later the raccoons invaded the corn plot in the dark of night. A new moon was just a shining sliver among the stars. No one saw the critters shuffle across the road or file in from the pasture behind the house. No one heard them rear up to sample first one ear of Early Sunglow and then another.

By morning a few stalks were broken, a few ears ripped from their shredded husks. Grim-faced, Mrs. Flint showed the children the damage. It was time to turn on the big lights and sound.

The electrical cords were already in place. Mr. and Mrs. Josephson had added floodlights to vary the effect of Mr. Baring's spotlights. Kate's parents, informed by Kate that they were expected to provide the noise, had borrowed their sons'

portable sound system and some of their loudest CDs. "Anything for the cause," they explained to the boys, who wondered why their parents wouldn't dismantle their own stereo instead.

After that, Flint Farm Road sounded as though it were holding an all-night party. Mr. and Mrs. Flint had to move out of their bedroom to the far side of the house so they could get some sleep. Mr. Torpor, who already slept at the back of his house, didn't have another bedroom to move to. He stood the din for one deafening night and then asked the Flints to turn down the volume.

It took awhile to get the lights and sound effects regulated so that they didn't keep people awake but did keep the raccoons away.

Some of the neighbors began to wonder whether all this fuss was worth a few weeks of Flint Farm corn. Then Early Sunglow ripened. The ears were picked before the sun rose high. They were placed in the shade of the apple tree. Everybody saw to it that the corn stayed cool until it was shucked and dropped into boiling water. It seemed to all of them that it was the best corn they had ever tasted.

Just when Early Sunglow was all picked out, Honey and Cream turned ripe. The raccoons kept to the other side of the road or else to other cornfields, away from the lights and noise.

Early each morning the children helped pick the ears at the peak of their sweet fullness. They learned how to test the brown-tipped corn silk and how to part the husk just enough to sniff for ripeness. They learned how to break off the ears with two hands so as not to injure the stalk and spoil the other ears that were not quite ready for picking.

One Sunday morning after picking, Mrs. Flint invited the children into her kitchen and served them corn fritters for breakfast. They were hot and puffy and full of corn goodness sweetened with maple syrup. After that Mrs. Flint shooed the children out of the house so that she and Mr. Flint could get ready for church. The children scattered to their own homes, where they pestered their parents to get hold of Mrs. Flint's recipe for using yesterday's corn.

But most families never had any leftovers. They just ate and ate. It was almost as if they feared that the raccoons would overrun the plot before the brief corn season was over.

August waned and September loomed. So did school. The small green apples on the big tree grew rounder and began to turn red. The children made the most of their last days of freedom. They built a summer house out of finished cornstalks and set it around the backs and sides of the scarecrows. Although the roof kept caving in, the house did look like a real shelter. It made the scarecrows look like a family setting out for a stroll.

The children gave Starshine and Sunglow their first change of clothes since the raccoon invasion. Now they wore fall outfits, in keeping with the brisker weather.

Foster announced that the baby was to be called The Little Kernel. He gave Mr. Torpor full credit for the name. Ben tried to borrow Daisy's doll to put in the carriage, but his mother caught on and stopped him. Next he had the idea of getting Daisy herself to sit in the stroller for all the Sunday-afternoon drivers to see.

Daisy wanted to walk. When Mr. Addario heard her yelling, he came running after them. But as soon as he started to bring her home, she yelled even louder. She didn't want to be rescued. She wanted to stay with Ben.

Once she was set in front of the scarecrows, she played contentedly with the plastic baby toys. She even let Ben tie a bib on her head for a hat.

For a while Ben showed her off to all passersby. "My sister," he called out to them. When Daisy grew restless and began to fuss, he informed people that she was The Little Kernel and that she belonged to the scarecrows.

Kate tried to get Bramble to sit with her, but Bramble wouldn't stay in the sun.

After a while Daisy slumped down in her stroller and stuck her thumb in her mouth. So they decided to take her home. Ben pushed the stroller while Foster and Kate walked alongside to wave off any cars that might come too close.

22 By *the time* school started, the corn plot had lights and a sound system, a summer house, and a resident couple with a baby carriage. The school bus came so early in the morning that the children had to leave the picking to the Flints. Platinum Lady ripened and was harvested, followed by Golden Bantam and Miracle. Seneca Starshine and Peaches and Cream matured at the same time.

Almost every day Mr. or Mrs. Flint drove a truckload of sweet corn across town to the farm stand. And every day the bushel basket under the apple tree brimmed with fresh, green-sheathed ears. Sometimes one or two apples landed in among the corn. The can hanging from the lowest branch had to be emptied two or three times a week.

The Flints decided to see whether the raccoons had learned their lesson and would stay away from the plot. Some of the most glaring lights were disconnected. The sound was turned down, although not entirely off.

Days went by without any trouble. Across the road the field corn grew and grew. It was almost ready to be cut and chopped and stored in the silo for the cattle. A few tall stalks did fall to the raccoons, but the corn plot sounds and lights must have carried over to the big field. Or else the raccoons were waiting for the perfect moment when the field corn flavor was at its best.

After a while no one gave much thought to the critters. Mr. and Mrs. Josephson hosted a barbeque. They roasted ears in their husks until the kernels were just slightly scorched and gave off a smoky sweetness no one could resist. Ben's parents spent weekends freezing corn on the cob so that they would have it in the middle of winter. Foster's father and Adele made a corn pudding that was almost as good as Mrs. Flint's fritters. And Miss Ladd stacked up jars and jars of corn-and-pepper relish.

Only Mr. Torpor did nothing special with the corn, or at least nothing that anyone could see.

23 As *the first* real frost iced the open fields and pastures with a silvery glaze, the last of the corn, Golden Queen, began to ripen. Geese honked overhead. Apples thudded to the ground. Bittersweet thrust its wiry tendrils over fences and along the stone walls, its yellow fruit still round and tightly closed.

Mr. and Mrs. Flint were getting their field corn in. The raccoons must have smelled the freshly chopped corn as it shot into the hopper. One Thursday night they struck again.

In the morning Mrs. Flint gathered up all the good ears and also the ones from broken stalks that might still be sold. She was afraid that turning up the sound and lights wouldn't put off the raccoons now that they had found such easy corn.

"What would work?" asked Ben that afternoon.

Mrs. Flint shrugged. "Maybe if the lights blinked. Something different like that." But she didn't have time to stand and chat. There was the rest of the field corn to get into the silo.

The children blew on their hands to warm them.

"Some people have Christmas lights that blink," Ben said.

"Who?" asked Kate.

Ben didn't know. He had just seen them somewhere.

"We could let the raccoons have what's left," said Foster. "And tell Mr. Torpor," he added, "so he can come and watch."

"Watch the raccoons eating the Flints' corn?" Kate was horrified. "They've probably already had their share. Remember, it's one for the blackbird, one for the crow, one for the raccoon, and one to grow. How can Mr. Torpor want to watch raccoons pigging out on corn everyone's worked so hard to save?"

"He hasn't even worked that hard," Ben said.

"How do you know?" Foster shot back. "There's lots you don't know."

That silenced the other two for a moment. Then Ben came up with a challenge. "How about seeing if Mr. Torpor will check down here in the middle of the night? That way he could watch the raccoons and stop them at the same time."

"I don't think he goes out at night," Foster answered. "He reads and watches television. He likes nature stuff."

Ben and Kate exchanged a look.

"Moving lights!" Kate declared.

"Television!" Ben shouted. "The perfect thing."

They practically had to push Foster up to Mr. Torpor's door. He didn't look happy, even after Mr. Torpor asked him in. It was clear to Ben and Kate, who waited behind the hedge again, that Foster's heart wasn't in what he was supposed to get Mr. Torpor to do.

"What if he won't?" asked Kate.

"Then we'll borrow your family's," Ben replied.

By now Foster was inside the house. After a while Ben and Kate came out from behind the hedge. They waited a little longer. Then Ben said they'd better find out what was taking so long. Standing close together, they knocked on the door.

Eventually it opened. There was Foster with a streak of green paint in his hair. He seemed surprised to see Kate and Ben there. "Mr. Torpor can't come right now," Foster told them. "He told me to say that to whoever was at the door, unless it was Miss Ladd."

"Well, what about his TV?" Ben demanded. "Will he lend it to the corn plot?"

"I forgot to ask," said Foster. "We got busy."

"It has to be set up before dark," Ben reminded Foster. "We have to know if he won't so that there's time to get someone else's."

"Okay," Foster answered. "I'll talk to him."

Kate said, "You don't have to call us unless he won't. Okay?"

Foster nodded. "Okay."

Kate couldn't help adding, "Have a good time."

Suddenly he grinned at her. "I will. I always do."

She could tell that he was aching to get back to the painting, or to whatever it was he did while Mr. Torpor worked on his pictures.

24 *Foster remembered* to speak up about the television, but he forgot to be home before dusk. He tried to explain to his father, who had to come and fetch him, that darkness came so early these days it was hard to keep in mind. His father said he must also keep in mind that he shouldn't bother Mr. Torpor.

At Ben's house, Mr. Addario had come home early. First he gave Daisy her bath, and then he read to Ben and Kate. It was that book about children who drift out to sea in a boat. Even though Ben and Kate had heard it often before and Ben had read it to himself, they hung on every word. Thoughts of raccoons and corn never crossed their minds again that night.

In the morning they remembered. They met at Foster's house and nearly woke the grown-ups.

"Did Mr. Torpor lend his TV?" Ben demanded.

Foster, whose mouth was full of Shredded Wheat and banana, nodded.

"Don't you want to see if it worked?" Kate asked him.

Foster swallowed. He reached for his jacket and followed the other two out the door.

The children reached the corn plot before Mrs. Flint came out to pick. They could see at once that the Golden Queen was undisturbed. Not only that, but Starshine and Sunglow, bulky in their fall clothes, were back in the plot. Surrounded by dried-out stalks and empty husks, they appeared to huddle together as if to keep warm. They seemed content to gaze at the television screen that faced them from the edge of the plot. They were watching cartoons.

Mrs. Flint appeared and switched off the TV. She said she would turn it back on when the sun went down. She looked at Foster and said, "The late-night movies were a good idea. It does seem to have worked."

Ben drew a breath. "We all thought up the TV."

"I'm glad you did," Mrs. Flint told him. "And I'm glad the season is nearly over so we don't have to think up any new ways to outwit the raccoons."

Since there wasn't enough of the Golden Queen to take to the farm stand, Mrs. Flint gave the children big paper bags to carry home extra ears. On the road they talked about coming back in the middle of the night to watch the raccoons getting scared off by the television. Tomorrow was Sunday. That meant there was a chance their parents would let them stay up late.

"They'd be more likely to say yes," said Kate, "if someone older would come with us."

"Like one of your brothers?" asked Ben.

But Kate saw no point in asking them.

"How about Mr. Torpor?" Foster asked. "After all, he doesn't have his TV to watch, and he did want to see the raccoons."

Kate and Ben gaped at Foster. He didn't usually speak out like this.

"Okay," Ben finally responded. "If you invite him."

"I will," Foster said. "You two get some chairs. Maybe if we all sit with Starshine and Sunglow, the raccoons will think we're a part of the scarecrow family."

Kate told Miss Ladd about the plan to go late at night to the corn plot. Miss Ladd donated a kitchen chair and offered to provide a thermos of hot cocoa to keep the viewers warm.

Mr. Flint let Ben borrow an old milking stool and a wooden tub that could be turned upside down for a seat. "How many visitors are you planning on?" he asked.

"So far just us three and Mr. Torpor, if he'll come. We need a grown-up to make it all right."

"I doubt you'll see many raccoons with the four of you there."

"We'll be very quiet," Ben told him. "We won't even whisper."

Mr. Flint shrugged. "Myself," he said, "I've always believed nights are for sleeping."

"That's all very well," Mrs. Flint put in, "but maybe that's why the nocturnal critters have always been so keen on our corn. They come and go while we sleep through their raids. And now deaf old Bramble sleeps through them, too." She added that she would cook up a batch of popcorn and leave it in a tin on the porch. "To go with the late-night movie," she told Ben.

When all the parents understood that Mr. Torpor had agreed to walk the children to the corn plot and stay with them there, the three were allowed to go this one time.

Foster said he and Mr. Torpor still had some last-minute things to do. Mr. Torpor would get him over to Ben's house so that later on he would only have two house calls to make to gather the three children.

Kate got everything ready that she would need—a flashlight, her ski jacket, and the alarm clock, set for a few minutes before midnight. After that, all she had to do was wait. And try not to sleep too soundly.

25 *The moon* was so bright they didn't need their flashlights after all. It felt strange walking along Flint Farm Road with Mr. Torpor leading the way. Single file, he had insisted. If the raccoons were in or near the corn plot, they were less likely to be alarmed by a line of silent visitors than by a whole spread of them looking like one big beast. Kate thought Mr. Torpor, long-legged and stooped, might even look to the raccoons like some giant crane or heron.

Any night sounds they might have heard were smothered by the television that blared from the corn plot. That is, until all of a sudden tires squealed, as if bearing down on them from ahead. Mr. Torpor waved everyone over to the side of the road. But even though the squeals got louder, no car came.

"It's the TV," said Ben. "It must be a movie."

Mr. Torpor stepped back into the road. The children fell in line. They were almost there when Mr. Torpor halted again and beckoned to the children. This time he guided them to the far side of the road. Kate thought he must have seen something over in the big cornfield. But when she looked up the moon-drenched slope, all she could see was rows and rows of stubble.

Then she heard Ben gasp. She whipped around toward the scraggly corn plot. What seemed at first to be an assortment of small light bulbs strung unevenly in front of the television set turned out to be eyes. Kate stared. The eyes stared too, all of them fixed on the screen they faced, which Kate and the others could not see from this side of the road.

All three children and Mr. Torpor were riveted as they began to make out more than the light-bulb eyes peering from the black-masked raccoon faces. Some of those furry faces were partly hidden by moon shadows, but the ones up front became clear. Every stool and chair was crowded with raccoons. Four of them took their ease in the baby carriage as they watched the late show.

After a while Ben tried to look beyond them at the remaining stand of corn. When he asked the others if they could see any raccoons among the stalks, they hushed him. He didn't think a soft voice would reach the raccoons through the movie racket, but he settled back to watch the TV viewers.

Meanwhile Mr. Torpor took out his sketch pad and pencil. His head bobbed as he glanced across the road and then down at the paper on his knee.

The children could only imagine what was showing on the screen. Not, thought Kate, anything her parents would let

her watch. Too much violence, from the sound of it; lots of shooting and chasing and crashes.

But the raccoons were an ideal audience. The action held them so tightly in its grip that they didn't even stir when commercials came on. They seemed just as fascinated by cures for baldness and places where car mufflers could be fixed without waiting.

"They sell different kinds of stuff late at night," Ben murmured.

Kate nodded without speaking. She was watching a late arrival, a big raccoon with three smaller ones in tow. Like us, thought Kate, like Mr. Torpor and us. The raccoons waddled down the middle of the road, pausing from time to time as if they were looking over the seating prospects. The smaller raccoons stared straight at the people, but not with alarm. The bigger one chittered at them and drew them down into the midst of the viewers.

There was some kind of skirmish. Then one raccoon clambered up into Starshine's arms. Another scrambled onto Sunglow's shoulder, only to find there was nothing to grasp inside the jacket. This raccoon slid around, hung upside down, and then dropped to the ground to start over.

As soon as the newcomers were settled in with the other raccoons, Mr. Torpor stood up. "This could go on all night," he said. "It's time for us to go home."

"We forgot Mrs. Flint's popcorn," Ben protested.

"I forgot Miss Ladd's cocoa," Kate added.

"No," said Mr. Torpor, "I did. Miriam Ladd brought it over

before I came to get you. We'll stop at my house and have some to warm ourselves up."

So they all trooped up to Mr. Torpor's, where light shone out of his windows onto the road. But that was not all. The inside of his house looked bright and welcoming.

They found the front room full of people. Mr. Baring had brought a card table, whch was set up in front of the windows. Mr. and Mrs. Josephson had brought a pot of corn chowder to put on the table. Kate's parents had come with a standing lamp and a cake from their freezer, which was only partly thawed but very festive. Mrs. Flint had brought hot mulled cider along with her tin of popcorn. Miss Ladd poured steaming cocoa into mugs that Mrs. Addario had brought so that no one would use wasteful paper cups.

The children were so astonished that it took a few minutes for them to realize that the front room walls were no longer bare. Pictures spanned the long wall across from the windows, pictures of corn, larger than life. Each was painted to look like a seed packet; each showed an ear with its own kind of kernels and its exact name. But here and there, almost hidden in each picture, a few small critters could be seen, like a corn borer crawling around from behind an ear.

"This is a regular gallery," Mr. Josephson declared.

"We'll have corn all winter," Mrs. Flint exclaimed, "one way or another!"

On the end wall there were smaller pictures of the various critters that had visited the corn plot.

Mr. Torpor pointed to a red-winged blackbird. "Foster did

that one," he said. "And this turtle over here. And these two others."

Everyone studied the critters on the walls. Kate was drawn to one showing ants carrying a leaf, with giant corn shadows overhead. It gave her a feeling of what it must be like to exist in that tiny corn-plot world.

Mr. Torpor drew Foster aside. "I know I should have asked before putting up your pictures. But it would have spoiled the surprise part of our surprise party."

"That's all right," Foster told him. "But can I still sometimes paint in here?"

Mr. Torpor nodded. "I'm going to. There's better light than in the kitchen."

All around them, people talked about the wonderful feast and about the pictures and about the raccoons being so hooked on television that they had forgotten all about the corn they had come to steal. Then the grown-ups thanked Miss Ladd for getting them up for this party and thanked Mr. Torpor for having it in his beautiful picture gallery.

"Yes," said Miss Ladd, adding her soft clear voice to theirs. "Thank you, Frank, for being such a willing partner."

Mrs. Flint reminded everyone to stop by in the morning for the last corn of the season. Then Miss Ladd handed each person a jar of her corn-and-pepper relish to take home.

AFTER

The next morning Mr. Flint had to turn off the TV because Mrs. Flint overslept. There was no sign of the raccoons. And not one ear of Golden Queen was disturbed.

Later that day Sunday drivers and their passengers noticed a great change in the Flint Farm corn plot. The TV was gone. So were the extension cords and lights.

The scarecrows themselves were no longer to be seen, at least not as they had come to be recognized. Instead, leaning up against the apple tree were one old broom with most of its bristles gone and one bedraggled mop, its head matted in limp, gray locks.

"Someone might want them back," Mrs. Flint explained to the children. "The handles can still be used for something."

"A good thing, too," Ben's mother confirmed. She was glad that nothing had been wasted during the long battle for the corn.

No one objected to Mrs. Flint's offering: a few discarded

ears spread invitingly on the overturned wooden tub. Everyone agreed that the raccoons might be extra hungry after spending a whole night in front of the tube. It seemed only decent to share these last ears, especially those with kernels just shy of ripe. Enough corn for a taste, Mrs. Flint remarked, but not so much as to raise any false hopes among the critters about next year's crop.